The Backside of the Clock

By

JW Kelley

The Backside of the Clock

Manufactured in the USA
Create Space Independent Publishing Platform
North Charleston, SC

ISBN: 9798801281162
LCCN: 2022909059

Novels by JW Kelley

The Strange Adventures of Brent and Bonnie Blue

When the Devil Comes Calling… (The Trilogy)

24th Precinct/The Heartsick Killer

The Backside of the Clock

Night Riders of Sheridan

Five Vets and a Funeral

Yesterday's Tomorrow

The Astronaut's Twin

Shadows in the Dark

Corporal Gallagher

Smile of Affection

Dreamer's Market

Dog-Eared Books

Manny and Ralph

Starbucks Corner

Cyclotron Factor

Words & Phrases

Long Way Back

Sunday Edition

Fortune Teller

Pages in Time

Novels by JW Kelley

Two Buckets

Mind Reader

Curious Tale

Laundromat

Will Power

$38 Billion

Killer Five

Time Loop

The Novel

Mukaluks

Desert 91

The Attic

Alley Cat

Stranger

Code 99

Howard

Conjure

Castles

Publications may be purchased online

Barnes&Noble.com

KindleBooks.com

Amazon.com

CHAPTER 1

The tranquility of the research facility, situated in the corner of the antiquated building, was opposite of the once thriving machine shop. Today, it was a mere skeleton of what it was during its heyday as a bustling manufacturing business. The dilapidated structure had been vacant for years until purchased for a pittance by three teenage geniuses who converted a portion into a scientific laboratory.

Currently, secret experimental trials were being conducted thus, the area was blanketed with a reverent hush as the trio of scientists worked silently. They moved about like ballerinas preparing to perform the seven sequences of ballet for the Bolshoi Academy in Moscow.

However, this triad of researchers were not ballerinas, but extraordinary prodigies, who wore starched white laboratory coats and were on the verge of a significant scientific discovery worthy of an Alfred Nobel's Pulitzer Prize.

For nearly seven years, these three Postdoctoral Fellows had experimented, tested, and analyzed the nature of time while observing and recording all data in this unique field of study. And in so doing, they produced a self-contained, oblong, metal device they termed, '*The Backside of the Clock.*'

The three-physicist designed, refined, and manufactured a capsule capable of transporting the occupants into the fourth dimension, as published by Jean le Rond d'Alemberts, Dimensions, followed by Bernard Riemann documentations. Their central concept was that the past and future are traveling therefore, they must exist. Time is distinct from space but in the fourth dimension. This machine recognized time as a progression of events from the past to the present and into the future as if turning a page in a novel.

The device utilized an onboard nuclear power-breeding modular reactor capable of producing 600 MW of electricity, which is the exact amount of energy required for the apparatus to catapult the occupants into the fourth dimension of time and space, thus to a different period... and there's the rub. That point in time, be in the future, or past, could only be identified after reaching that destination.

Joyce Wilson, twin sister to her brother, John, were considered geniuses in elementary school.

The Taylor School principal called Wilson's parents in for an unscheduled teacher's conference. After arriving, they were immediately escorted to the principal office, where Mr. Gonzales, motioned for them to enter.

"Well, what have they done now?" quizzed Mr. Wilson as his face flushed scarlet while gritting his teeth.

"Have they skipped again?" asked the woman as she wrung her hands nervously in her lap.

Gonzales shook his head negatively and smiled. "Heavens no. They are remarkable students, and it's a pleasure having them in our school. However, that is not why I've asked you in," the man squirmed in his seat before continuing.

"Okay, let's have it!" ordered the father leaning forward.

"Do either of you have a university degree? I'm only asking for professional reasons?"

"No, but we did graduate from high school," stated the woman, followed by a weak smile of accomplishment.

"Well, we've taken the liberty of testing the twins."

"And?" questioned the man sternly.

"I know they are only in the third grade, but our counselors believe, as do I, they should move into high school as soon as possible. And most likely, they will only be there briefly before moving into a university setting where they will be able to receive a proper education."

"High school, college? For God's sake!" exclaimed the mother, "They're only babies, and I know they're smart, for they've been reading since they were two years old."

"We can't afford college," snapped the father rubbing his ruff-callused hands together as if trying to start a fire.

The principal smiled again while leaning back in his chair. "The state will pay for all expenses. You are lucky, Mr. and Mrs. Wilson, for you will be able to select any school of your choice, and have all expenses paid. It may be advisable to have an educational counselor assist you with your selection. Nowadays, it is not just the higher learning aspect that is important, but the institution they attend, for example, Harvard, Stanford, MIT, Oxford, to name a few."

The principal office became library quiet as the three adults sat in muted silence in understandable confusion.

CHAPTER 2

The third member of this triad was Eddie Washington, born in New York City to a dark-skinned father who had immigrated from Jamaica and a pale white mother with wallpaper blond hair from Scandinavia. They met and immediately fell in love while working at the United Nations.

Their relationship resulted in an offspring they named Edward, who could almost be called beautiful with skin the color of golden bronze, light-colored hair, and a muscular physique.

He was asked numerous times to engage in various sports while in school; however, he refrained. Washington was a quiet, patient, and modest young man, not given to emotional displays but with a natural shyness that made him avoid accolades and attention. He could be silent to the point of being inscrutable, making it difficult even for his closest friends to gauge his moods and desires. He used most of his free time for academic purposes to study and perform in-depth research.

Nonetheless, his greatest asset was his IQ of 172, which is considered in the genius category. He graduated from high school at age nine, Leland Stanford Junior University, age twelve, where he met the Wilson twins with similar intellect and desires. The three completed their various Ph.Ds. in the scientific realm of study, and the rest is history.

The prodigies turned and grinned at each other, for they knew how close they were to the ultimate breakthrough. All of the relevant data had been collected in their quest for time travel and this knowledge was ready to be tested.

Joyce was five feet 10 inches tall, statuesque, as was her brother, John. Both had disheveled dishwater blond hair, fair complexions, azure eyes and were considered nice looking. Her brother, John, was occasionally brusque and aloof, yet charming and gentle among friends and loved ones, especially Joyce.

"We know what we place in the capsule travels somewhere," stated the 19-year-old woman sternly, glancing from one teenager to the other.

"But where?" questioned Edward, the other 19-year-old, scowling. "But where? Everything we place in it disappears after the capsule returns. Hell, it may just disintegrate, leaving nothing but molecular dust!"

"That's true, Joyce," entertained John, stepping back from his computer.

"Why does the capsule return and not what we placed within the protective sphere?"

"Because it has gone, '*Where No Man Has Gone Before,*'" returned John, chuckling paraphrasing the Star Trek TV series.

"Yeah, but where, Captain Kirk?" asked Edward.

"As William Shakespeare so eloquently stated in Hamlet, when his character was contemplating suicide, *'To sleep; perchance to dream: ay there's the rub for in that sleep of death what dreams may come?'* "And for us, where is the rub... and I repeat, where is the 64-dollar question of the day?"

"I should have become a physician and I'd be making money hand over fist instead of laboring in this stinking lab for a pittance," complained Eddie.

"Yeah, but who would consult a teenage doctor who doesn't even shave?"

They all laughed at the comment.

"You could have become a pediatrician, and then you could have played with your patients."

The twins snickered again, but Eddie just smirked.

The three teenagers hugged each other as they always did. It was a nervous reaction to the situation they knew, but their clutching together calmed them.

"If we go forward in time, will we age? Or if we travel back, will we get younger?"

The boys laugh at the female part of the team. "John and I will get more handsome either way we go, but you, on the other hand, will probably go the other way."

Joyce immediately picked up a book and threw it at the other two while grinning but did not hit them on purpose. "Brats!" she bellowed, smiling at her good friend and brother.

CHAPTER 3

Edward cleared his throat before talking, for he was adrenaline-charged and wanted to control his voice. He took a long slow breath to calm himself, and his anxiousness began to dissipate.

"Time is nothing but a construct." After a prolonged duration, he continued. "We have successfully created a device, utilizing this small, fast-breeding modular nuclear reactor producing 600 MW of electricity which is enough to power a city. However, it also yields a gravitational wave. And as we know, a gravitational wave is a ripple in the fabric of space and time, which has been our ultimate goal all of these years, thus, opening this door and allowing us to enter!"

"But?" started John.

Eddie held up his hand. "We are at the pinnacle of our time travel experimentation. But before we continue on this historical path, we must consider, if successful, the various consequences of our journey. For example, the Grandfather Paradox: anything that happens while traveling should logically make your original time-travel trip impossible. However, if you were to kill your grandfather in the past, you should never have been born in the first place, therefore, you could not have traveled to the past to kill your grandfather. Or the Butterfly effect: a situation in which an action or change that does not seem important yet has an enormous effect."

"Both of these conclusions are strictly speculation and written by persons who have never time-traveled; therefore, they are unproven theories," interjected Joyce.

"They did not utilize the scientific testing method for verifying, and evaluating," stated John.

"True. However, it is still something we should consider if we're successful."

"How will we ever know if we don't try?" asked John picking up a Coke, drinking it, after which he dropped the empty tin can into a waste container.

"We are utilizing an untried digital operating system with a reactor that could blow us all to hell and gone along with half of the city. But if it does work, where will it transport us? To the future or past and how far and for how long?" She put his hands on his hips, tilted her head, and waited for an answer.

"Or, as I said earlier, will it turn us into molecular dust?" questioned Eddie Washington. "Not playing the Devil's advocate, mind you," he continued watching the other two for a reaction.

"There is only one way to find out," stated Joyce smiling at her two colleagues.

"I have an idea." Joyce pulled out an old pocket watch from a handbag she sometimes carried. "I suggest we place this in the capsule, turn it on and wait to see what happens to the watch."

"Whose watch is it?" asked John, knowing full well it was their fathers.

"Dads," she returned with a devilish smile.

"He'll croak if he discovers we took it."

"We won't tell him."

John shrugged his shoulder and stated, "Okay."

"Do we dare take anything with us?"

The three youngsters grinned at each other.

Washington walked over and turned on the power grid, looked back, and nodded to the twins as they placed the watch on one of the confined spaces within the capsule.

Joyce flipped the ignition switch, and a moment later, the building began to shake as if there was an earthquake. There was a kaleidoscope of glittering fragments, and within a split second, the capsule began to shake, rattle, and roll like a carnival ride along with a deep rumble. There was a massive explosion as the immense power was unleashed in uncontrolled fury.

At the same time the machine's software began to manage the system as the lights started to blink and the various mechanisms started to hum.

There was no way to anticipate the emotional impact they were feeling at that exact moment. Their heads turned as they watched the complex control terminals winking and blinking, messages back and forth as they communicated with the other electronic devices throughout the lab. Several bulbs turned various colors, some becoming brighter and then dimmer.

And then silence.

"Well?"

They carefully opened the hatch.

The golden watch was partially smashed, leaving only *The Backside of the Clock* in tack.

"So much for that theory," joked Washington picking up the now broken watch and examining it. "Maybe you should return this thing?" he said, jokingly.

Joyce shook her head and smacked him lovingly on the shoulder.

"Now what?" asked John looking more perplex than usual.

Silence.

CHAPTER 4

"We are too close to stop now. Forget the watch. It may have been a fluke?" stated Edward as he paced back and forth in the room.

"How will we ever know if we don't try?" asked John.

Each of the teenagers looked at each other.

"Okay, but what should we bring with us?" asked Joyce.

"Ah, Farmers' Almanac?"

"Sports winners throughout history."

"Copy of the top songs for the last several decades."

"A handful of diamonds."

"All the greatest stocks in history."

"Formulas."

"Book on inventions."

"Designs, blueprints or diagrams for various electrical apparatuses."

"And the list could go on forever."

"How about a hard drive with everything we have listed... and more?" asked Eddie.

"We would have to take a laptop computer," interjected the woman.

"Would a computer work in the past, future, or whenever if we're not dust?"

"We'll be transported by an electrical jolt that could send our hearts into asystole or ventricular fibrillation as well as wiping the hard drive and computer clean, thus making them only useful as a bookend."

The three looked at each other and waited for several seconds.

"But a hard drive and a laptop seems like a good idea whether or not it works."

The smaller and more powerful, the better!"

"Agreed," the other two echoed.

Edward sat back again, took a deep breath. He paused, the lab was soundless. He rotated in his chair, looked at each of his friends, and said, "Each of us will take three items which they feel important. We don't have enough room for much more gear or anyone else for that matter." He projected a toothy grin.

Joyce and John bobbed their heads in agreement.

John raised his hand. "We still have most of our inheritance in the bank. Diamonds are a good idea, for if we were to make it, we'll need some currency."

"I've got 1300 dollars in my checking account."

"We should clean out our bank accounts, get the three items you decide to take, and probably write a note to our loved ones."

"Buy as many loose diamonds as we can and settle on a date," said Joyce.

"Should we tell anyone what we are going to do?" asked Eddie.

"No!" the twins answered in unison. "They would think we're crazy and want to watch or something."

"What about the lab?"

"It's been ours for several years. I will have all of the utility shut off and pay any outstanding bills. Perhaps we should tell our parents we are going on a sabbatical or something?" said Eddie.

"Yeah, otherwise, they'll worry themselves to death."

"If this thing works, I'm not sure we will be coming back anytime soon."

"Someone will ultimately search the lab and see everything, but no one will understand it. Notes or letters may be a good idea if we are gone... ah, forever into the past or future... or become molecular dust."

The three giggled.

"What should we do then?"

"Each of us has to make his or her own decision."

"One other thing," started Joyce. "What should we wear?"

"Something simple and not anything that stands out would be the best idea whichever direction we go. Thus, no logo T-shirts or anything flashy like Michael Jordan Nike Air sneakers. Everything should be plain as possible is my theory."

"Maybe a light, non-descript jacket could come in handy?"

"I speculate we'll end up here where we started, but in a different time."

"Should we bring a weapon or weapons?"

"I have a Glock 19 Gen 5 9mm 15-round pistol at home," said Eddie. "Though it's never been loaded or even fired."

"I don't even know what all of that means," said Joyce shaking her head.

"It's a handgun, but that's a good question. What would happen if we ran into some bad things or bad people?" put in John, bobbing his head. "I vote you bring it, but you better learn how to use the sucker first."

"Yeah, okay."

"Bring this, don't bring that, do this, don't do that. We're not going on a field trip, guys; we're going to travel in time! Take or don't take! Sunday at 0430, we launch come hell or high water!"

"What about medicines, antibiotics, or aspirin, Band-Aids. A book on emergency medical care could come in handy."

"We will all meet here next Sunday morning. Bring whatever you think is necessary and do what you need to do before we travel."

"Until Sunday, travelers."

Giggles.

CHAPTER 5

The air was heavy with anticipation as the three sat in a semi-circle, looking at the others. The friends appeared outwardly calm, but their hearts were pounding like jackhammers with excitement.

Eddie sank back in his chair, pulled a handkerchief out of his pocket, and mopped his brow. "I'm kind of nervous," he said; in a high-pitched scratchy voice.

"We all are," stated the twins in unison.

"Did anyone besides me bring a camera?" asked Joyce.

The other two nodded their heads.

"What time is it?" asked Eddie.

"Whatever time it is, we're wasting it." John glanced at his Apple watch.

"I put on my old Seiko," said Joyce, "it runs forever. It's 0435 and time to go."

They got up, picked up their travel bags, and walked over to the capsule. The trio stood trembling, young hearts racing. They looked at the machine they had spent years perfecting.

Eddie Washington, John, and Joyce Wilson entered their time machine's capsule and sat down. Eddie slid his bag under the seat and put on a seat belt.

"Put on your belts," he ordered, to which the others complied. "Just in case?" He smirked.

The crew, now strapped in, watched as Washington prepared for ignition. He turned and looked at the twins and they nodded as he made several last minutes adjustments.

The Wilson twins watched as Eddie Washington pressed the last button.

There was a kaleidoscope of glittering fragments, and within a split second, the cabin's capsule began to shake, rattle, and roll like a carnival ride along with a deep rumble. There was a massive kick in the back as the sound of immense power was unleashed in uncontrolled fury.

A moment later, the computer's soft wares began to manage the system as the lights started to blink and the various mechanisms started to hum.

There was no way to anticipate the emotional impact they were feeling at that exact moment. Their heads turned as they stared at the vast array of complex control terminals winking and blinking, messages back and forth as they communicated with the other electronic devices throughout the lab. Several bulbs turned various colors, some becoming brighter and then dimmer.

And then silence.

"We're not in Kansas anymore, Toto," one whispered. The words hung in the air like an Oregon fog.

CHAPTER 6

"Is everyone okay?" asked Joyce, her taut voice breaking with excitement.

"Good here," replied Eddie.

"Same," echoed John. "I thought this thing was going to be torn apart for a while. Where are we? Does anyone have any ideas?"

"When are we, would be a better question?" stated Joyce. "Still in New York by the looks of it. But not anywhere close to our time."

"It's getting dark."

Within the apparatus, it reek from body odors produced by excess nerves and warm bodies.

"I'm sweating like a pig," said John.

"We should get out," suggested Eddie.

They slowly opened the door, looked about, got out, and stretched. "I feel like someone beat me up," said Eddie rubbing his shoulders.

"Yeah, me too," repeated John.

The machine landed on a field of grass and garbage, near several beat-up tin sheds. It appeared to be on a bluff about thirty feet above a nearby river. The lip of the bank looked down on a marshland below. But on the other side of the estuary were hills of green.

"Help me push this thing into that gully over there. Hopefully, no one will see it there. But be careful not to push it too far, otherwise, it may go into the stream."

After several minutes of struggling, the trio moved the time machine into the deep brush, hidden and out of sight.

"There's the skyline, though it's certainty's not our time, that's for sure," Joyce said, pointing a crooked finger toward the city's lights several miles away.

"There's a bunch of stores a couple of blocks away. Let's go find out when we are."

Meanwhile, down the road a crowd was gathering on the other side of the street close to a shop of some sort.

"Over there. See at all those people ganged around that storefront. I wonder what they're doing? Wait, I think, ah, I think they may be listening to a radio or something? Jesus, they are. Let's go see what's up."

There were several stores across the street, including a general type of store with an old-looking wooden Philco radio sitting on a chair in front on the walkway. The crowd was staring and listening to a radio. They waited intently as to what was about to be said.

The radio station announcer stammered, his voice crackled from nervousness but quickly regained his composer and started. "President Roosevelt is about to speak."

"Christ!" barked Eddie. "I know what he is going to say. Yesterday, December 7th, 1941—a date which will live in infamy—the United States of America was suddenly and deliberately attacked by naval and air forces of the Empire of Japan."

After a few short minutes, the president stated to the listening audience:

"Yesterday, December 7th, 1941—a date which will live in infamy—the United States of America was suddenly and deliberately attacked by naval and air forces of the Empire of Japan."

The crowd of nearly 25 listeners turned and stared at the youngster, shocked at what they heard. First, the teenager stated what the president would say, followed by Roosevelt echoing the same rhetoric.

"How did you know that?" asked an elderly gray hair woman moving toward the teenagers.

"Yeah, kid, how in the hell did ya know what he was gonna say?" questioned a big blue-collared workman with hands the size of baseball mitts. He stepped so close to Washington, that Eddie could smell what the man had eaten for lunch. "Well?" he graveled as the other people looked and waited. "Are you a Jap spy or somethin'?"

"Ah, ah, we better go, guys!"

The three travelers turned and quickly rushed down the street toward the city center.

"I guess we better watch out what we say. But we know it's December 1941, and it's cold as snot here."

CHAPTER 7

After several hours of walking, they made it to the city center.

"We need to search for the diamond district," said John.

The others agreed, and they began to look.

"Hope the stores are still open."

"This is New York City. They're always open," put in Joyce.

"We need to sell the diamonds and then buy or rent a place for us to stay."

"Joyce, we think you should do the selling, and feel free to use tears."

"Why me?"

"You're a young woman, and women cry. Tell them your grandmother died and left the diamonds to you in her will. And lower your head and sob, and while sobbing, "tell them your grandmother raised you, and you're very sad and can't believe she died."

"Oh, brother!" complained Joyce. "Well, okay," she relented.

The plan for Joyce was to go into several different jewelry stores and sell a couple of stones in each one. Therefore, no one would get suspicious... hopefully.

"You never know what people will think with a teenager selling expensive diamonds. If they ask, say what I said. Your grandmother left them to you when she died or something along those lines," said John Wilson as the other two watched.

"Okay?"

"How much should she ask for?" asked Eddie.

"As much as we can get. And then will find a betting establishment so I can make a wager."

"On what?" asked Joyce.

"January 9th, Joe Louis will box Buddy Baer and knock him out in the first round. Hopefully, someone will take my wager when I put the money on Louis winning in the first... otherwise?"

Several hours later, they met at a café and went in to have coffee. The waitress and asked, "may I help you?"

"Coffee latte grande," replied Eddie.

"Make that three," said the other two.

The elderly waitress stepped back and tilted her head. "What's a latte grande, my young friends? If ya want a cup of java, it'll cost ya a nickel. So, do ya want a coffee or not?"

"Please, ma'am, three coffees."

The woman stomped away, shaking her head and mumbling to herself.

"I just..."

"We all just..."

They giggled again when they paid 15 cents for the three coffees and left a dollar tip.

The travelers sold most of the diamonds and had nearly $94,000, but it took them most of the evening and the next day. Several store owners questioned where they got the stones, but when Joyce started to cry while relating how her grandmother had died and left them to her, the store owners purchased the stones.

The two boys were glad they decided to let the girl go into the jewelry stores and do the selling, for it worked only after shedding the tears. Joyce sold the entire diamond collection for a total of $93,768.

"Well, now what?" she asked, sitting down on the grass.

"A room for the night, supper, and maybe a couple of brewskies."

"Yahoo!" they chanted.

"But only order what's on the menu."

They chuckled at Eddie's joke.

CHAPTER 8

Eddie took 30,000 dollars and wagered it on the Joe Louis and Baer fight. He bet Baer would be knocked out in the first round... and was. Thus, Washington doubled his money, but the men who paid out the enormous winnings were furious. Eddie hurried off as fast as he could, racing down the block until the establishment was out of sight, but he glanced over his shoulder until he got back to the hotel room they were renting.

After searching for several days, they found The Beresford Apartments in the middle of the block. It was a luxury, 23-floor "pre-war" apartment building at 211 Central Park West, between West 81st and 82nd Streets, on the upper West side of Manhattan in New York City. This majestic complex looked ideal for what the trio had in mind. Buy and allow their apartments to be rented until they return... if they ever did.

"What we need," stated John is a family-type lawyer!"

"Why?" asked his sister.

"Because if we plan on coming back here in how ever many years, who knows, we may need a trust or something to prove we own these apartments."

"Huh?" vocalized Eddie. "John may be right!"

There is a bank building on the corner, and those types of businesses always have lawyers somewhere around."

Twenty minutes later, they were sitting in a very regal office with numerous books on the shelves and degrees nicely framed and hanging on the walls.

"Mr. Jenkins will see you now," said the lawyer's secretary displaying a fake, well-used smile.

"What may I do for you three?" Asked the kindly elderly man behind a gigantic oak desk near the window.

Edward stepped forward, cleared his throat, and started. "We are going to purchase three apartments at the The Beresford. They are located..."

"Everyone knows where the Beresford is located, young man," he charged back somewhat, irritated. "What do you want with a lawyer?"

"We need a trust describing the three apartments and us as owners, but more importantly, we want to give them to our grandchildren or who we feel should get them." Edward moved back and sat down beside his colleagues and waited.

"How can you three afford such expensive real estate?"

"That is not your concern, sir!" put in Joyce.

"Hmm!"

"Very well. We will set you up with three trusts. They are similar to a will. If you earn money renting them, the proceeds will be deposited into a trust asset account at a local bank. The said assets will gain interest as long as it stays in the account. You may describe how to manage the property, upkeep, and such. The trust assets will have your names printed with specific instructions as you desire. When presented, there will be no doubt who owns the properties. Any questions?"

They shook their heads negatively.

"They will be ready tomorrow at 10:00 a.m. Please see my secretary and she will show you out." Another fake smile.

They purchased three two bedroom, two-bath, furnished Beresford condos overlooking Central Park for nearly 32 thousand dollars each, which they paid in cash by their new lawyer, Mr. Jenkins. He bent over backwards to accommodate the trio after they presented him with a bonus of one thousand dollars to make sure everything was perfect.

The real estate man looked at the trio curiously, but after Joyce sobbed long and hard, and explained their grandmother left them the money, he handed her his handkerchief.

Mr. Jenkins sealed the deal with the titles, insurance, and all of the necessary paperwork needed in New York City.

The condos closed quickly, for the sellers wanted their money, as did the real estate salesman.

"Congratulation, Mr. Washington, Ms. Wilson, Mr. Wilson," said the lawyer and salesman.

"In 2022, these places could be worth millions," said John grinning with the other two.

"Well, today we got them for a lot cheaper. Maybe we should buy another for investment purposes?" replied Eddie with a toothy smile.

"How much do we have left?" asked Joyce.

"Close to 60K and change. What I won on the fight."

"I'm glad we put in the contract that the real estate company could rent and care for them and deposit the money into our trust accounts."

"Maybe we'll go look at the condos when we stop traveling."

"Enough about fiancé, let's go eat; We're starving," the men stated."

"Don't make me start to cry again," joked Joyce,

They all laughed.

"Food is dirt cheap, and so are hotel rooms."

"Yep, so now what?" questioned Washington.

"We should probably do some intense planning."

CHAPTER 9

The three started to meander toward Times Square, where numerous people were wandering up and down the street.

"Let's go eat over there," said Joyce, her finger pointing where a crowd was waiting. A sign on the business read, *Sloppy Joe's Soft Drink Stand.* "Must be good otherwise; there wouldn't be a long line."

"Okay," the boys answered, already walking across the street toward the stand.

John stopped and looked up at a theater marquee. The sign read *Tales of Manhattan, starring Charles Boyer, Rita Haworth, Ginger Rogers, Henry Fonda, Charles Laughton, and Edward G. Robinson.* "Maybe we should take in a movie; it might be fun."

"Let's eat first; I'm starving."

"You're always starving," answered her brother.

"You two act as if we are on vacation or something. We're in 1942. 1942, people. Our parents are not even born. There is a terrible war ragsing, which the Japs started when they bombed Pearl Harbor and will continue until 1945, with thousands of people dying as we stand here eating a Sloppy Joe's sandwich. And you're thinking about seeing an 80-year-old movie."

The twins stopped eating and stared at Eddie Washington. "What do you suggest we do?" one asked.

"Yeah, what should we be doing?" questioned the other.

"Something productive rather than going to see a movie."

"Why don't we go over to Central Park finish these delicious sandwiches, discuss the situation and decide. I've got a couple of ideas if you two agree?"

Several minutes later, the three teens sat on a bench to discuss the situation and ate.

"It's kinda chilly," said Joyce.

"Yeah, let's go to our new homes and eat there. It will be warmer," returned another.

Their new condos were warm, cozy, and well furnished. The building was relatively new in 1942, as was the furniture. The previous titleholders were getting a divorce, and the other two needed the money soon, and wanted to settle as quickly as possible, thus the excellent price, but it was still expensive during this time frame. The other owners must have been wealthy, for the furnishings are of the highest quality for the 40s.

"Whose condo is whose?" asked Eddie. "Or does it matter?"

The other two shook their heads negatively.

"I like um all," said Eddie between mouthfuls.

The others bobbed their heads in agreement.

After a while, John, Joyce, and Eddie sat gazing out the window at the view, which overlooked beautiful Central Park.

"These are my thoughts. We should go to several of the largest business in the city, like IBM. Is IBM even around now?"

"Yeah, they've been around since 1911 or so."

"How'd you know that?"

Eddie shrugged his shoulders and said, "Cuz I'm gifted."

They all laughed again.

"Anyway, think of it this way. We are before the internet, hell, before Apple, Microsoft, or Google and we know things that could benefit all of mankind now and forevermore."

"I turned on the computer, and it works just fine, except there is no internet, which is okay. We brought it to use for what's on the hard drive, not for Facebooking or surfing the web."

CHAPTER 10

"What's troubling you, Dr. Washington?" questioned Joyce as she carefully watched the man who seemed out of sorts for some unknown reason.

"We don't belong here," he whispered, his voice faint with words falling before they reached her.

"What do you mean we don't belong here?" asked John now concerned with the interaction between the other two.

Washington's head swiveling around owl like as he repeated, "We don't belong here!"

"You're scaring me," said Joyce scooting closer to her brother.

The atmosphere in their apartment suddenly became tense, with the only sound being Edward's foot-tapping the floor that echoed throughout in the room.

Washington turned away, squeezed his eyes shut, took a deep breath, and repeated for the third time, "We don't belong here!"

"What?"

"God did not play dice with the universe. Space is woven together with time into a single fabric; Because of our desires, we pried open that composition revealing threads of dangling particles of the nonspatial continuum."

"What in the hell is that?" asked John.

"We interrupted the irreversible succession from past, present to future and all it encompasses. And that, my colleagues, is the rub."

The hair on Joyce's forearms and the back of her neck stood upright. She started to get up, but it was too late for her and the other two.

Something out the window caught their eyes, and they all turned as if hand puppets on a string. The trio felt the world changing before their eyes. But without their time machine.

The light of day seemed to fall out of the sky and sink into the wine-dark waters, where it disappeared into the blackness of nothing.

"I'm scared," mumbled Joyce.

"We all are, Joyce," said John, holding tight to his sister's hand.

CHAPTER 11

There was not a single sound nor a speck of light, or any discernable movement to be seen by the terrified teenagers. There was nothingness... and they were caught up in it.

"Is this the cessation of our life or existence?" asked Joyce in a squeaky voice.

"Total nothingness is death," stated John as he held tightly to his sister.

"We're not dead!" barked Washington

"Well, if we're not dead, where are we?"

"ay there's the rub."

"You're always quoting Shakespeare!"

"When are we?" whispered Joyce into the blackness. "Can you guys see any stars?" she asked, looking up.

"It's cold," one stated, shivering.

A cold numbness was quickly enveloping them as they began to think they might die from exposure and dehydration.

Suddenly, a rush of wind, flickers and flashes of light in all directions and a loud screaming noise.

"What are you three kids doing out here in the garage? And why are the lights turned off? For goodness sakes, children, it's dark and cold out here. Get in the house this very minute before you catch your death!" ordered Mrs. Washington. "And besides, it's time for lunch. We have baloney sandwiches with milk and Famous Dave's sweet pickles. Hope you like them as much as we do." The tall slim blond woman laughed at her joke as she shooed the youngsters into her home.

"Go wash your hands, you three!" ordered Mr. Washington from the front room reading the newspaper.

The three kids raced to the bathroom and started to wash their hands.

"Well, geniuses? Now, what?" queried John. "Did your folks notice we're no longer children?" He continued.

"Well, we go in the kitchen and eat baloney sandwiches with milk and Famous Dave's sweet pickles like my mom told us to."

"You have to admit this composition of threads of dangling particles of the nonspatial continuum is strange."

"It may be strange, but I think we should do as Eddie's mom said... and besides, I'm hungry."

"Me too," the other two echoed.

"One question?" asked John.

"Okay," answered Joyce.

"Do they know how old we are now or are we back being kids again?"

"God, I hope not."

"Mom," started Eddie as he ate his sandwich, "how old are we?"

"Edward Washington, you are the same age as Joyce and John, of course," she smiled motherly and continued to eat.

"How old is that, Mrs. Washington?" asked John.

"Why you're all nine years old and just graduated from high school. And the good news is you will all be attending Stanford Junior University next month and hopefully will graduate with honors... if you study hard!" She beamed as a proud parent should while patting Edward's arm.

"Thanks, Mom," said Eddie.

Turning to the twins. "To me, you two look like our normal 19 years old selves, but to mom, we are ten years younger. That is so odd. I wonder how long we'll stay here?"

The others shrugged their shoulders, not knowing the answer.

They wiped their mouths and took their dishes to the sink. "The baloney sandwiches, milk, and Famous Dave's sweet pickles were pretty good," stated one of the nine-year-olds.

"If we stay here long enough, I hope we get some more baloney sandwiches, milk, and Famous Dave's sweet pickles."

Two smiled, but Joyce could not help but laugh at her joke.

"Ah...

"We're going again!"

"We feel it too."

"I'm scared!" mumbled Joyce as she clutched tightly to her brother's arm.

The hair on Joyce's forearms and the back of her neck stood upright again. She started to get up and say something, but she could not speak or move, for it was too late.

"Hang on!" someone screamed.

The world began to change before their eyes as Washington's kitchen disappeared into oblivion of nothingness.

The next second, they were gone leaving nothing, but molecular dust and a hollow echo.

CHAPTER 12

"Excuse me please!" snapped an irritated, middle-age woman. She was forced to walk around the three people standing in front of the gaping doors of the elevator as they clunked open and partway shut, while attempting to close, but without success.

"Sorry!" the three apologized together.

"Now, where are we?' asked John

They all looked around. It appeared as if they were in a hallway on the 77th floor with a bank of elevators and stairwells going up and down. It turns out there were 99 elevators and all busy going up and down the 110 floors.

"Ma'am, we are lost. Could you tell us where we are and the date?"

The woman lowered her glasses and asked, "You don't know where you are or the date? Are you three youngsters on drugs or something?"

"No, we are just new to the city and are lost. We are from overseas," said Joyce.

"Well," she started, "today is September 11, 2001, and it's..." she checked her wristwatch, "it's 8:34, and you're in the North Tower of the World Trade Center."

"Oh, my God!" they all voiced simultaneously.

"What's wrong?" she asked now concerned as her face paled.

"We have to get out of here as quickly as we can. A plane is going to hit this building in less the eleven minutes.

"Should we take the elevator or stairs?"

"Stairs!"

"Take off your high heels, lady, and follow us!"

In the next instant, the four of them were racing down the stairwell as fast as possible. They shouted warnings at everyone they saw along the way down, "A plane is about to hit the building. Get out!" Some did, some did not.

The next thing they knew there were more than twenty people were racing down the stairs with them as fast as they could, toward the tower's ground floor of the tower. One young guy raced by them but waved over his shoulder.

"What time is it?" asked Joyce, nearly out of breath.

"8:44."

"Get ready to hold on!" shouted Edward.

The 20 people burst out of the building just in time to look up and see the huge plane about to hit the North Tower.

"Oh, my God, you were right!" one person shouted as they all raced away from the coming storm of wrath and destruction from the plane and falling debris.

On September 11, 2001, at 8:45 a.m. on a clear Tuesday morning, an American Airlines Boeing 767 loaded with 20,000 gallons of jet fuel crashed into the North Tower of the World Trade Center in New York City.

The impact left a gaping, burning hole near the 110 floors of the skyscraper, instantly killing hundreds of people and trapping hundreds more on higher floors.

The 20 runners continued out and away from the mass of destruction unfolding but still followed the three teenagers.

"Keep going; in a few minutes, another plane will hit the other tower. Hurry! Get as far away as possible!" yelled Washington over his shoulder,

Eighteen minutes after the first plane hit, a second Boeing 767 United Airlines Flight 175 appeared out of the sky, turned sharply toward the World Trade Center, and sliced into the south tower near the 60th floor. The collision caused a massive explosion that showered burning debris over surrounding buildings and the streets below.

The group watched in awe and hugged each other, knowing the three teenagers had saved their lives.

"Thank you, Joyce, Edward, and John," said the cranky middle-aged woman they had met on the 97th floor, "but how did you know?" she asked.

The question was ignored. Washington started to move further away. "Get back!" again, warned Edward, "this tower will collapse!" All eyes watched as the South tower swayed slightly collapsing into a massive heap of rubble.

The people gathered around the three teenagers one asks, "Who?"

"Islamism militant terrorist. A group called al-Qaeda."

"But how?"

"Put a cloth over your mouth and nose. The dust can be deadly, and move back as far as possible."

Everyone was now covered with grime, dust, and dirt as smoke poured out of the North Tower. People around them were yelling and crying while holding onto each other. Billowing smoke and flames could be seen from miles round.

The group looked up just as a shirtless man leaped to his death rather than be burned. A moment later, another was seen leaping out of the building. The sight was indescribable as each person took a collective breath of the horror they were witnessing on this day.

At 9:59 a.m., after burning for 56 minutes, the South Tower of New York's World Trade Center began to collapse down onto the street. The group, police, and pedestrians ran for cover. Everyone was covered from head to toe with dust, ash, and dirt. Most were coughing and hacking.

At 10:28 a.m., after burning for 102 minutes, the North Tower of the World Trade Center collapsed.

More dust, smoke, and ash filled the air engulfing the surrounding area dissolving the World Trade Center from view by the people below. Everyone was in shock and despair at what had happened.

People were still coughing as they held different types of covers over their noses and mouths.

"Thank you again for saving us," said the shoeless woman who they had met in the stairwell. "But how did you know?" she asked again while tilting her head and rubbing dirt from her eyes.

The three visitors walked away without another word as all of the group watched them leave.

"How did they know?" another asked.

CHAPTER 13

"What now?" asked Joyce, while looking at her two colleagues. The men shrugged their shoulders and shook their heads as to what they were to do next.

"I don't think we should stick around here," stated Edward looking back toward the crumpled towers. "Too many questions and not enough answers."

The three travelers felt a tingle signaling them to immediately grab hold of each other.

"Something is happening again. Do you two feel it?" were the last words out of Joyce's mouth?

Joyce screamed!

John yelled, "Hold on tight!"

"I am!" echoed Edward as he held John's other hand as hard as he could.

The trio appeared to tumble about in time and in slow motion as if in a bowl of Jell-O. And just as quickly they landed sprawled about on the ground like children's pickup sticks.

"Where are we now?" asked Edward looking about in the unfamiliar place.

"As Dorothy said to her dog, Toto, I've a feeling we're not in Kansas anymore," joked Joyce scanning the area where they had landed.

"We're in the middle of a jungle of some sort, well not a jungle per se, but super thick vegetation that's for sure. We are high on one of the numerous hills that I can see. Below us looks like the tidal streams near those standing oak trees. Over there, in the low-lying area, is what looks like marshland among the many hills around us."

"We're still in New York. Mannahatta means the island of many hills and there are the hills everywhere," said Edward scanning the surroundings. "But what year... I have no idea?"

A deer meandered across their path and went into the thick forest of birch, ash, aspen and pine. A waterfall to their left plunged several hundred feet before crashing with a deafening roar.

"It's beautiful," said Joyce, wherever we are.

The three started down the hill following the river.

"I'm hungry," said Eddie,

"Wish I had a Big Mac," echoed John.

Joyce chuckled at her two fellow travelers.

CHAPTER 14

The time travelers looked down from a nearby hill toward what was now New Netherland.

"There must be several hundred people living there."

"They certainly dress weird!" said Edward as they watched with vivid interest.

"We're in the year 1600 according to history, and if so, this is probably New Netherland in about 1626," continued Edward Washington.

"Our four fathers," stated John. "It must be the New Netherland Company, as you said. That is when they were trying to kill all of the Indians, so they could take their land. We should find the Dutch merchant Pieter Schagen, for he was responsible for purchasing the island of Manhattan. Maybe they would stop the horrific slaughter if the Indians agreed to sell the island to the white man."

"Not very many blacks other than the ones working."

"They are slaves, I think?" said Eddie. "I'm not going down there otherwise, they'll hang me or something."

"You're probably right," interjected Joyce.

"Eddie, you should stay out of sight the best you can," said Joyce, as Washington nodded in agreement.

As the two entered the small Dutch village, most of the people turned and stared at them, for they were tall, blond, and dressed in clothes from 2022.

A teenage boy walked up to them and asked, "what type of attire do you wear, strangers?" he asked looking them up and down before they could answer.

"So much for not standing out?" joked Joyce.

A middle-aged man wearing breeches full at the waist, a doublet and jerkin, hip-length, and loose jacket with free-hanging sleeves. "Hello, I don't remember seeing you on the ship. I am the Dutch merchant Pieter Schagen, director of the West India Company and the exploration and settlement of New Netherland.

"We were hoping to meet you, kind sir. I have an odd suggestion for you, Mr. Schagen."

"And what may that be, young man?"

"There have been many killings on both sides. Indians and Englishmen; and I think you may be able to stop them?"

"How so?" he inquired, with a slight head tilt.

"We suggest you attempt to purchase this island of Manhattes from the savages, as you call them."

"They do not desire English pounds."

"True, but they would consider wampums such as axes, iron kettles, blankets, and wool clothing. They are excellent traders. So, it is best not to cheat or offer beads, or trinkets etc." continued Joyce

"It is far better to bargain with these people than killing all of them," stated John in an authoritarian tone.

"What makes you think they would take such a paltry sum for their land?"

"They do not wish to fight you, for you have the long muskets which they fear."

He nodded his head and listened to the suggestion.

In the distance, there were three-gun shots from Edward Washington's 9 MM Glock. All turned toward the noise.

"We must go. Think about our suggestion, Mr. Schagen." They turned and sprinted back toward the hilltop where Eddie was hiding.

They arrived back to the clearing, and saw Eddie holding his Glock at the ready.

Three trappers were on their knees, hands behind their heads, all sweating profusely.

"I'm glad your back. These guys thought I was a run-away slave and raised theit muskets to shoot me or take me back to the village of New Netherland below. I disagreed and fired three shots in the air and told them if they did not drop the weapons, I'd shoot them next. Well, they did what I ordered. But they did ask where I got the magnificent repeating pistol."

About this time, the earth started to shake violently making it difficult to stand up. The travelers were thrown to the ground. The trappers rolled over on their sides but tried to reach their long muskets.

"Don't do it!" ordered Washington.

They immediately looked up and stopped squirming about and trying to get their weapons.

In the distances, they could see the ground and hills rolling... and the next moment, the three travelers were gone leaving the trappers lying on the ground, unharmed but pale with fright.

"Where'd they go?" one asked as he picked up his musket and surveyed the area seeing nothing but a swirl of dust.

"We better not tell anyone what we saw. No one would believe us if we told them about the repeating pistol or the three people disappearing into thin air."

They nodded their heads and started down the incline to the village of New Netherland in 1626.

CHAPTER 15

"Where are we now?" asked the feminine voice of Joyce Wilson, who was still clinging tight to her brother's arm.

"Wherever it is, it's cold as snot," returned Edward Washington as he looked about the area though could not see much in the dim light.

"Wait, I see some people walking toward an old, dilapidated building," whispered Joyce.

"Jesus, it's us!" said John in a low voice filled with excitement after recognizing the other three.

"What should we do?" inquired Edward turning back to his comrades.

"I don't know," answered Joyce.

"Neither do I," countered John.

"Well, crap! What year is it?"

The only sound was the deafening sound of silence and their pounding hearts.

"We've got to go over there and find out what we are about to do?"

"What will happen if we touch us?" asked Edward.

"We'll probably explode or something. Why would we touch our other selves?" joked John.

"Shake hands, a hug, I don't know," he answered while shrugging his shoulders.

"No one knows? Because we are now here with those other three in a parallel existence that has never happen before in human history. Thus, no one's knows the ramification when the six of us meet. But we will not explode."

"Okay, let's go see what the other us are doing," added Joyce, smiling.

The three got up walked to the laboratory and peeked in the dirty window. The other three were jabbering back and forth about what to take on the exploratory excursion in the machine.

"Well, shall we go in?" asked Eddie.

"Hell yeah," said John.

Joyce nodded her head.

They slowly opened the door. The laboratory was situated in the far corner of the old building that was once a thriving machine shop.

Today, the interior of this lab was blanketed with a reverent hush as the trio of scientists worked silently around a unique metal capsule. They talked and pointed, wrote various things onto an iPad, and appeared to be discussing something about the electrical current needed to power the device.

As the outside three entered, the inside three stopped working and turned as if marionettes. Not a word was spoken as each of the threes stared in shock at the others.

"Ah," started Edward, "the time machine works. Maybe too good."

"What? Jesus, your me, or maybe I'm you. I don't know what to say," said the inside Edward while gawking at the outside Edward.

"How did you get here?" they asked in unison.

"By that device, we've all worked on. Oh, by the way, it works except for a couple of hiccups."

"Hiccups? Like what?" Asked the inside Joyce.

"Well," started the outside Joyce, we have no way to guide or select the year we want to go. And once we travel, the object still carries us to other timelines, but without us entering the capsule... which is weird."

"How can that be?" asked the inside Edward.

"We don't know, but it does. It has the unique capability of traveling and pulling us with it," answered John. "Where are you in your experimentation phase?" quarried John, watching the other John standing beside the capsule.

"We sent off Joyce's dad's watch, and it came back broken. How did you get here? The capsule is here in front of us. And how can there be six of us?"

Joyce moved forward, but not too close to the others. "I don't know if we should touch or anything... we've all read the same books about that sort of thing, though there is no scientific proof of that hypothesis. Anyway, we are here to tell you what we've found so far and what has happened to us in our time traveling experiences."

"Okay," said the other John still staring. "This is so weird!" he continued shaking his head."

They all grinned.

"First of all, we must get into your capsule," said the outside three. "If we don't, we'll be taken to hell and gone again by the gravitational wave which has taken several times before and without the time machine."

"What?" questioned the other Edward. "How can that be?"

"We don't know, but we are caught up in this gravitational wave or ripple in the fabric of space and time, which opens wormholes that somehow drag us even though we're not in the craft. Somehow, we are still connected to the wave.s As you know, wormholes are a hypothetical warp in spacetime permitted by general relativity. Our time-travel machine hypothetically used this traversable wormhole to initiate the electrical propulsion system. We expected to be brought back to our original point of origin, but unfortunately, we found out that once this wave is started, it can carry you all over without any means of terminating the time travel."

"But?"

"If you are ocean surfing, you catch a wave or not, sometimes the power of the ocean pulls you back rather than sending to the beach. It picks you up and throws you wherever the wave decides. And that is where we are, caught in a time displacement wave that has taken us all over, but finally we made it back here to our lab. We must get back in the capsule and perhaps the wave will no longer be able to tumble us through time."

The six scientists stood looking at each other, trying to make heads or tails of everything that had or would happen to them.

"Where are you in your experiments?" asked Joyce

"We were about to get in the time capsule and power the device, hoping it won't blow up the city."

"Well, don't; otherwise all of us will be forever bouncing from one time to another without any means of stopping. We need to be able to set a designation."

"How? Questioned John.

"We don't know. However, maybe we can figure something out."

"In the meantime, we are getting into the capsule, and hopefully it will stop us from being taken by the next wave."

The three quickly opened the hatch and crawled in and shut and locked it securely.

About this time, the ground started rumbling and shaking like a popcorn popper.

"Here it comes, you guys," the three inside the capsule screamed as they lowered their heads to protect themselves just in case something bad happened.

"What should we do?" asked the three standing outside the capsule.

"Hold on tight!" yelled Washington.

"How long will this last?"

"Not too long... we hope," followed by silence.

After the shaking stopped, everyone assumed it was over. However, it was just the beginning. The aftershocks were as severe as the initial tremors.

From inside the metal time-travel capsule, the three looked at each other.

"Well, it didn't get us this time. Do you think it was because the device protected us?" asked one.

The other two nodded their heads as they looked out the machine's portal.

"Look!" gasped John, "our capsule."

Sure enough, on the floor of the lab was the first-time machine.

They crawled out, and the six of them stared at the other mechanism.

Suddenly there was a huge explosion, and smoke filled the lab. The time-traveling metal capsule had somehow disappeared along with the other three people leaving the original machine and the original three.

The atmosphere was hot, close, and tense as the three searched the area.

"Jesus, where'd they go? Are the dead? Now, what?" asked one.

"They are not dead otherwise..."

Joyce sucked in her breath audibly, "Otherwise we would be dead too... I think," answered Joyce.

"Poor bastards," returned her brother.

Edward was telling himself it could not be true, all the while knowing it was. They were gone. "You don't fool with Mother Nature," said Edward Washington

"Now what?" asked Joyce.

John sat down and looked around the deserted laboratory.

Washington sat down beside him. "We must find out how to steer this thing and set a date where to travel."

"How?"

"As I said earlier, time is nothing but a construct. Our little pod pried open the fabric of our reality, revealing dangling bits of our world in different time zones. These particles are the woven thread of the fabric of space-time and matter bends space, and space directs how matter moves."

"Well?"

"That's all I know. We must learn how to direct space," said Eddie seriously.

"We'll get right on that, Edward."

They all grinned.

"Now, this is really weird," stated Joyce.

"What?" the other two asked.

"There are our three travel bags we started with," said Joyce.

They searched through them revealing everything they had started with including, the diamonds, hard drive, laptop computer and Washington's Glock 19 Gen 5 9mm 15-round pistol.

The trio stood trembling, young hearts pounding not knowing what to do or think.

"Were back where we started, troops."

CHAPTER 16

The trio of inventors had been working on nothing but the steering and destination mechanism for the manned cylindrical time machine for nearly six months. They came up with a digital system capable of navigating in a three-dimensional environment of time, place, and distance. Like an underwater submersible with rudder controls side-to-side or yaw and diving planes. The alignment of descent or pitch needed to be adjusted constantly. However, this was for waves of time and not the ocean.

The system's software included the documentation by video and still cameras. The new capsule also had oxygen sensors, outside temperatures thermometer, and a GPS for radio waves. Also incorporated were an oxygen generator and CO2 scrubbers to completely sealed-off the capsule from the external environment if necessary.

"I think we're close," said John, wiping his brow of perspiration.

"I think so too," added Washington.

"Well, I don't know? Once we try it and it goes where we want, I'll be more optimistic, but until then?" put in Joyce.

"When should we try?" asked Edward leaning against the wall.

"Tomorrow morning?" questioned one.

"Well, why not?" interjected John, grinning.

The following day they all arrive before 6 a.m. with smiles. They took an inventory of what was in the cylindrical metal capsule. They had a first aid kit, hatchet, folding knives, water, an ax, hunting knives, lighters with extra fluid, a tent, water filter and purification tablets, space blankets, a folding saw, compass, and multiple fire starters for the cooking stove. Also included were three Glock 9mm pistols with three hundred extra rounds.

"Do we need three Glocks? We're time traveling, not hunting," questioned Joyce shaking her head.

"Yes," both men answered.

Part of the gear was placed in the backpacks, while the rest was stored behind the seats and any open space not in use. s

"I think we're ready," said Washington.

They closed the hatch tightly, buckled in, and glanced at each other.

"Ready," said Washington.

"Ready," said John.

"Ready, said Joyce.

Washington dialed in their destination, turned on several switches, and looked at his colleagues. They nodded.

He grinned and pushed the starter button, which ignited a rumble culminating in a deep throbbing roar that was felt as well as heard. The lights in the lab started blinking on and off, followed by a thunderous cracking noise as if the sky was breaking apart. The time machine and its occupants disappeared in a bright flash.

CHAPTER 17

Outside their portholes, they could see the sun's rays bouncing off freshly fallen snow and could tell it was bitterly cold outside their time-machine. The only noise was the howling wind slicing down the snow-covered slopes of ice cover tundra as the strong winds blew from the North.

"Hey, we're surrounded by ice and snow in every direction!" exclaimed Joyce. "Where did you take us?"

"I don't know?" answered Edward looking at his calculation. "Oh, man. I may have added a zero or two when I plugged in the time links. We may have gone back a further than I wanted... a lot further!"

Joyce screamed as she stared out one of the view openings. "Jesus!" she shouted, moving back and pointing.

The other two quickly peaked out and saw a man covered in furs sprinting toward them as fast as he could run, for right behind him was an ugly beast the size of an elephant chasing him. It had a giant mouth full of sharp teeth chomping as it tried to eat the man.

Joyce threw open the hatch just as the man got closer, allowing him to dive through the opening, after which she slammed the hatch shut.

The man, short in stature though thickly built, had pinched eyes from the frigid temperature, thick callused hands griping a heavy wooden spear he held at the ready even though he was on all fours after jumping into the capsule. His eyes were as big as saucers with fright as he quickly surveyed the area. He rubbed his beefy arms in a futile effort for warmth while moving his short, muscular legs together as if marching, hoping to steer the heat to his feet.

The man muttered something under his breath, no words, just growls as he stared at the time-travelers. His chest, waist, and legs were wrapped with reindeer hide cut and sewn together with braided woolly mammoth strands. His enormous shoulders were draped with the thick coat of a Gray wolf. Stitched together and covering all was the skin of a walrus, providing essential protection from the harsh elements of this ice age. His feet were bound with the thick pelt of a giant tundra mammoth secured by shaggy hair from the beast. Over his makeshift boots were more of the waterproof coat of the walrus. Around his thick waist was a rope made from the same walrus which held down the fur. Slipped tightly beneath the waistband was a 16-inch tusk weighing just over a pound. It was crudely decorated with various scrapes and cut marks but had a menacing sharp point. His hairy face had scraggly black tresses tangled together that shifted back and forth as if alive when he moved his large round head. A rather prominent nose dripped with each struggling breath while nostrils puffed thick fog. His agate brown eyes blinked back at them.

"Arrr," he roared, his voice sounding like crushed gravel.

John put out his palms and lowered his head momentarily. "John," he said, touching his chest. "John," he repeated, palpating his chest. He then pointed to the caveman, who said nothing.

The caveman glanced about the machine but kept a tight hold of the spear. He looked out the porthole and jumped back, for the beast was still there looking at the device.

"Oga, Oga!" he growled, nodding his shaggy head toward the large beast while thumping the lance on the steel floor of the time machine.

"John," he repeated again touching his own chest and then pointing to the caveman who said nothing.

The man tilted his head slightly, thumped his chest like Tarzan, and rumbled, "Irock!" He again hit his chest and repeated, "Irock."

"Maybe he's hungry?" said Joyce, looking him over.

"Give him an MRE," said Edward.

"Okay," and she dug out an MRE, unsealed the package and opened all of the canned meats and beans. She took out a coke and popped the top. Joyce handed the food to the man, but he just looked at it.

"Eat," said Joyce taking the fork and taking some of the meat. "Eat."

Irock carefully took the food, examined it, and took a small bite. "Yuga," he mumbled between bites as he shoved the food into his mouth as fast as he could with his fingers.

Edward showed him how to drink the coke, which he chug-a-lugged, followed by a loud belch and a grin.

Oga, Oga!" he growled again, nodding his shaggy head toward the creature outside while banging the lance on the steel floor of the time-machine.

They all peered out the view openings, and the monster was nowhere to be seen.

"Oga, gone," said Edward walking his fingers across the air.

"The caveman looked out and bobbed his head in agreement.

"Maybe we can help the poor man?" asked Joyce pleadingly.

"Why not?" answered John.

"Will we change history in some adverse way?"

"What?" asked one.

"The phenomenon whereby a minute localized change in our complex system could have a significant effect in the future or something like the Butterfly effect."

"I want to help him and to heck with the butterflies."

"We agree!"

They all started rummaging around behind the seats looking in their gear. They pulled out a huge hunting knife and scabbard, an ax, four MREs, lighters they demonstrated, two powerful flashlights and extra batteries, a folding saw, multiple fire starters, cooking stove and gas, along with a roll of duct tape. The trio also gave him one of their Glock 9mm pistols and an additional 100 rounds, after which they spent most of the day teaching him how to use the various items, but it was hard for him to understand the fire starters and gun.

After John shot an ugly giant rabbit that was no bunny, he cleaned it with the knife, and cooked it over the portable stove, it was then he understood and responded with another impossible-to-understand sound.

Washington pulled out his favorite black backpack and showed the caveman how to use it to carry his new treasures given him. The man shook his head in wonderment as he pulled and pushed on the rucksack's material, now full of the new possessions.

After several tries, he could slip it on without a problem. But he took it off again, pushed and pulled on the rip-stop durable nylon, polypropylene, and growled again. He looked at the three-time travelers and nodded.

Irock held the Glock in his right hand near his thigh and, after the many demonstrations, realized the danger it presented when the trigger was pulled as well as the usefulness it had to protect him from the numerous bad things roaming the area... and for hunting for food.

"Okay, Irock, we have to go," Edward did the airwalk again, and the man understood.

Irock stared at the three for several seconds, bowed his head, and grunted something they could not understand. He looked at the hatch and made the finger walk in the air.

Joyce opened the hatch, and the caveman crawled out and walked away wearing his backpack with all of his new possessions. The 9mm, however, was held firmly in his hand, as he marched away in the snow. He repeatedly turned back and nodded always grinning a picket fence smile.

CHAPTER 18

"**D**o you think we screwed up our future by giving Irock all of those things?" asked Joyce as she watched the man until he was out of sight. "It would have been interesting to see where he goes and how he lives."

"Well, what we've done is done," put in John as he too glanced out the other porthole. "That monster thing was scary as all hell!" he continued.

"Scary as all hell! What do you suppose it was?" inquired Edward.

"I don't know and I don't want to know. It was huge with a lot of teeth!" whispered one.

Why don't we dial up another adventure without big bad things?" giggled Joyce.

"I agree with my sister. No more bad things."

"You got it, troops," barked Washington as if an Army officer. He flipped the various switches in the time machine while keeping an eye on the blinking and winking lights that came into play after turning the ignition to on.

"Fasten your seat belts; it's going to be a bumpy night," he said, quoting Bette Davis' character, Margo Channing, in the movie, *All About Eve.*

The three smiled when they felt the familiar movement and rumble of their time-machine capsule.

CHAPTER 19

Washington and the two Wilsons were feeling the adrenaline rush as the chemical surged through their bodies while they watched their colleague make ready for another time-traveling adventure.

They all felt the pulsating pneumatic sensation of the machine, which was similar to India's most significant and wildest roller coaster, the Nitro.

They glanced at each other, now filled with pure excitement. The twins held hands.

The concept of the future is hard to define precisely. Still, a common element of such is that our society will be completely transformed from the present day to be almost unrecognizable. While the future cannot be predicted, our current understanding of the various scientific fields allows the prediction of possible future events, if only in the broadest terms. More people, warmer climate, drought, and the oceans rising.

And after a few moments, the time-machine capsule landed and settled. Where, God only knows, but the three occupants were stunned to see the future from their little world's portholes.

"Where are we now, or when are we now?" asked Joyce, still peeking out.

"We've landed on top of a building that looks as if it is made of some type of Acrylic, for I can see down several floor levels," said Edward. "Should we get out?" he asked, looking for guidance.

The other two nodded and said, "Sure, why not."

The rooftop was vacant except for them. The three walked over to the edge and gazed down. It was like looking at an anthill, for there were so many people they would be impossible to count, let alone feed or provide water or housing. And... it was extremely hot.

Edward took out a pair of binoculars and looked down at the millions of people. "They're all carrying large water bottles on their hips or sides. Strange," he mumbled to himself.

"It's 138 degrees," voice Joyce checking her thermometer.

106

"138 degrees? Holy crap!"

All of those people are walking on an elevated walkway, and there's water under them. I wonder if there was a flood?"

"That's the ocean," said Washington. "Global warming, along with the ocean rising."

"Jesus!"

"Exactly!"

CHAPTER 20

"I don't want to stay here any longer," stated Joyce walking back to the capsule.

"We don't either," echoed the other two.

In a few brief seconds, they were strapped in and ready to go.

Washington turned toward the twins and asked, "Forward or backward?"

One returned, "Forward."

The other said, "Backwards."

"I'll choose," said Eddie smiling. "Hang on, troops!"

And they were gone.

CHAPTER 21

"Where are you taking us?" asked the twins as they watched the pilot of their craft guide it into another dimension of time and space.

Edward dexterously operated the navigational system using the software, they had installed. The craft's new system could now travel into the fourth dimension with the machine recognizing time as a progression of events from the past to the present and into the future that could be directed to an exact location and timeline.

His eyes scanned over the digital readouts hoping the machine was going where he directed the capsule for this crucial mission, but he crossed his fingers just in case.

After a short duration, the metal capsule landed with a dull thud that sounded like metal on metal.

Eddie turned and looked at his partners in time crime.

The two tilted their heads and made faces. "Well?" they both asked.

"I think we may be on the White Star Line, RMS Titanic. The British passenger liner that sank in the North Atlantic Ocean on 15 April 1912 after striking an iceberg during her maiden voyage from Southampton, UK, to New York City. She had an estimated 2,224 passengers and crew aboard. More than 1500 died, which made the sinking one of the deadliest for a ship at that time. The Titanic was under the command of Captain Edward Smith."

"Titanic? The Titanic? Why? Eddie, this may have been a big mistake!" barked John with Joyce bobbing her head.

"Well, let's go see the Captain Smith and see if we can save some of those poor people?" he replied.

"Is this a good idea?" questioned Joyce.

"I don't know? But we can only find out if we try. Oh, a couple of things you should know. The Titanic strikes the iceberg at 11:40 p.m., and shortly thereafter water starts filling the ship. At 2:10 a.m., the ship's lights will go out and at 2:17 a.m., the ship breaks in two, and both halves sink."

"What are your plans, sailor Washington? Grab an oar and paddle?"

"Come on! Let's go find the captain and tell him what will happen."

The Wilsons shrugged their shoulders and got out of the machine.

"Where are we? It looks like we are somewhere near the engines or something. See all of that equipment, and the sound is deafening."

We're on the G-Deck, the eighth deck down from the top, which is the lowest on the ship. Sorry. I was trying to land on the top deck. Guess I need more practice!"

"Much more!" they all snickered.

The Backside of the Clock

CHAPTER 22

"Hey! What are you kids doing down here? You're not allowed in the engine room! It's off-limits except for the ship's crew!" yelled a burly man in worker's clothes.

"Who are you?" asked John Wilson, standing up as tall as possible.

"Joseph Bell, the Chief Engineering Officer of the Titanic," he barked, not used to being questioned as he placed his baseball-sized hands on his hips. "And you?"

"We are here to try to save the Titanic!" he returned, without a smile while projecting a firm face.

"What are you talking about? Save the Titanic?" he continued moving closer to the three.

"What time is it?"

The big man glanced at the clock on the wall. "11:22"

"After the *Titanic* enters Iceberg Alley. The air is clear, and there is no moon. The sea is calm; thus, nothing to give away the position of any nearby icebergs. At 11:39, lookout Frederick Fleet will spot the iceberg and notify the bridge, but it will be too late."

"What are you saying? You said your name is John"?

"Yes,"

"How do you know all of this, John?"

"Today, April 15, 1912, at 11:40 p.m., this ship, on her maiden voyage, will strike an iceberg on the starboard side, ripping a huge hole in the ship's steel plates of the hull, some 12 feet square opening it to the sea, and flooding the ship. At 2:20 a.m., the ship will break apart and founder leaving over a thousand passengers on board to die."

The man stood dumbfound listening to the teenager. "We must hurry and get to the Captain Smith and First Officer Murdoch!" he screamed.

"If I were you, I'd order your crew out of the engine room, for they will die first if you don't. This ship is going to sink in two hours."

The man flipped about, shouted several orders to the numerous men in the engine room, and raced up the stair toward the top deck and the bridge.

"I cannot. The crew knows what to do in case of an emergency," he yelled over his shoulder, looking down at the trio.

"They'll die!"

"We all die!"

"John, I don't know if we have time to make it to the bridge and back,' warned Joyce.

All eyes turned to the clock and it read, 11:34 p.m.

"If we go up those stairs," the three glanced at the steel stairs, "we'll get stuck up there and die too. We should return to the capsule and leave!"

"You've done all you can do in the limited amount of time," said Washington. "We should go now!"

A few minutes later, Edward, John, and Joyce hurried to their machine. A cute little Scottish Terrier with Incredibly short legs raced up, wagging its high set tail while looking up anxiously at the group. His raven-black coat was well-groomed and he wore a collar.

"Come on, Scotty! You better hop in otherwise... well, you don't want to know," said one.

"What should we do?" asked John, petting the dog while examining his collar. "It has his name on it! J.J. No, wait! J.J. Astor IV. Holy crap, it's John J. Astor's dog! He's one of the wealthiest people in the world at this time... but he dies today along with more than 1500 other passengers. Sad! So very sad! We tried to save them, but we are only able to save the Scotty dog," he continued still petting the dog but now displaying a sad, sorrowful smile.

"If he stays, he is going to parish along with the numerous people about to die. Let's take him home with us!"

The twins looked at Washington, who shrugged his shoulders and said, "Why not?" and grinned.

"Why not?" echoed the other two.

They all strapped into the time-traveling pod as Washington prepared to guide the craft to another time period and place.

They glanced out the portholes when they heard the loud screech of crumping steel and the hull buckling from being ripped open by the iceberg. The ocean water gushed in, covering the metal deck in a matter of seconds flooding the entire engine room.

The complement of courageous engineers, electricians, boilermakers, plumbers and clerk attempted to quell the influx of the ocean, but it was in vain. For moments later, the engine room became a watery grave for all and the unsinkable RMS Titanic of the White Star Line.

The ship sank during the early morning hours of April 15, 1912.

"We should go! I can't stand to watch any more of this," sniveled Joyce, wiping her watery eyes.

The two men turned away from the sight as the capsule began to rumble and shake.

Scotty dog whined.

A moment later, the time machine, three travelers, and one Scottish Terrier were gone.

CHAPTER 23

The derelict building had once been a vessel of the community with men and women working together producing a much-needed product. But now, after years of neglect, it was empty and dirty, with numerous stains on the windows and floors. It was a mere skeleton of what it once was in its heyday.

However, near the far corner, it was aseptically clean with a reverent hush as a large metal cylinder appeared out of nowhere.

The hatch on the side of the craft opened slowly and out jumped a black Scottish Terrier that immediately went to the corner and peed like a racehorse after the Kentucky Derby. And then he ran all over, stiffing here and there until he was satisfied with what he smelled.

"Lucy! I'm home!" and then Eddie Washington laughed at his poor imitation of Ricky Ricardo on the TV show *I Love Lucy.*

The other two crawled out of the capsule, stretched, and hurried to the bathroom.

After a week of rest, the three met back at the lab to discuss what was next.

"Where's Scotty?" asked Joyce to Washington. He's home sleeping, I guess, or was when I left."

"Why don't we see if our condos are still standing?" asked Eddie.

"We'll need the trust paperwork, IDs, and everything necessary to prove we own them... otherwise, they'll give us grief!" put in Joyce.

"Yeah, you're right. I have everything in a lockbox and I'll go and get it."

"Hey, that's a great idea," countered John.

"Well," started Joyce, "we've been gone for nearly 80 years their time. And I know we signed a contract to rent them out, but 80 years? Get a grip!"

"It won't hurt to go see, Joyce. Who know?"

"Okay, let's go see," returned the other twin.

They took a taxi to the subway station and hopped on the underground until they reached the Central Park area. They had to crane their necks to see the top of the new modern building surrounding the park. But there, in the middle of the block, at 211 Central Park West, was The Beresford, the 23-floor luxury apartment building.

"Is that our place?" asked John, staring.

"Yep, we bought 3 of them if you remember correctly. If they are still ours is anybody's guess. We'll soon find out."

They started to walk into the building but was immediately stopped at the door. A big man, dressed in all the fineries of a New York doorman, put out his hand and said, "I'm sorry, but you kids will have to leave. This complex is for owners only." He placed his hands on his hips, opened the door, and waited.

"We want to see the manager!" barked Joyce, moving up to the man and looking him square in the eyes.

"You want to see, Mr. Barclay?"

"Please."

Several minutes passed until a diminutive man, balding, tiny mustache, wearing a suit, came out of the elevator looking irritated. "What seems to be the trouble, Franklin?" he asked, looking at the three.

"These three, ah, youngsters demanded to see you, the manager." He stepped back and nodded toward them.

"How may I help you, Mr...?"

"Washington, Edward. My fellow owners, Joyce, and John Wilson. We own apartments 27A, B, and C." He presented the man with the trust and all of the required papers proving they were the said owners.

"We... we thought... we assumed?" he stuttered and blanched white.

"Perhaps you should call your complex's lawyer."

"Yes, yes," he was finally able to say after several minutes.

An hour later, two men dressed in suits, not looking happy, marched into the mezzanine and headed for Barclay. They studied every word of the documents, including their identifications.

"Well," graveled the older of the two. "It looks like everything is in order. You three are all doctors?"

"Not medical, Ph.Ds."

"Doctors, nevertheless. Well done, and at such a young age."

"Thank you," they said together.

"You have a great deal of money in your trust accounts from your apartments being rented this long of duration. However, it will take several weeks for the present occupants to move out." He looked at the three.

"Fine," said Joyce.

"About the accounts?" asked Washington.

"The bank is The First National of New York on the corner. Just give them your IDs, Doctors, and the account number, and they will tell you how much is there. You may take the cash, transfer it, or leave it. Whatever your desire. Your grandparents were very smart to invest when they did, for they made you very wealthy."

"Thank you, sir," they said.

Eddie, John, and Joyce stood in the cashier's line until they got to the front of the cashier's cage. Edward presented her with the IDs and account numbers. She checked her computer several times, flushed red, and hurried to the bank manager's office. Several minutes later, a rather large, middle-aged man, dressed in a dark suit, lumbered out also with an amber face.

"What are your intentions?" he asked sternly.

"We would like to find out how much money we have in our accounts?" returned John moving closer.

"You have 2 million, 783 thousand, 523 dollars, and 22 cents."

"Wow!" stated the trio in unison. "That is a boatload! Hold it for now, and we'll decide later what to do."

"Good!" he whispered under his breath.

"Let's go get a coke or something!"

"Yeah! And maybe a hamburger and fries."

CHAPTER 24

They rested for several weeks before returning to the lab and the time capsule. The day started innocently enough as the three entered and immediately went over to their invention.

Joyce took the dark tarp off of the machine, for it was always covered when not in use. They opened the hatch and looked inside. "Still smells like the ocean," she remarked.

Scotty, the Terrier, quickly jumped in and smelled all around the small craft. After a few minutes, he hopped out and explored the lab some more. They gave a chuckle while watching Astor's dog.

"Is his name going to be Scotty or JJ," asked Joyce.

"Scotty, I guess," said John reaching down and patting the dog.

"Well, where to next?" asked Edward Washington as he backed away from the other two and sat down on one of the old chairs they had scattered in the laboratory.

Joyce and John quickly joined him as they began to talk about various destinations they would like to visit.

Unexpectedly there was a loud banging on the metal door to the lab. They hesitated while looking at each other. Someone continued to bash on the door as if they were trying to break it down.

"Now, who could that be?" asked Eddie.

"Why don't we find out," stated John going to the door. He opened it.

"Will you please stop that damn hammering!" shouted John as he pulled the door open.

A small, elderly man, bent with age, who had difficulty speaking English was standing in the doorway. At first, he stood motionless and only stared at John with large, liquid soft, agate brown eyes. After a short time, he did his best to speak clearly, but his accent was so thick that it was difficult to understand.

"I am in desperate need of your services," he finally stammered with some difficulty. His raspy voice was just above whisper but had a desperate quality even with the heavy foreign inflection.

Edward and Joyce joined John, and the three stood together as if welded. John glanced at the other two and

128

said, "We do not understand your question... what services?"

The man again grasped for the right words. They could tell he was calm on the surface but was hiding a great turmoil. His eyes narrowed to a squint before he continued. He took a deep asthmatic breath and closed his eyes, "I am not a rich man, but what dollars I have are yours," followed by a wheezing exhalation.

"We don't want or need your money, Mr..."

"Ramadani, Besnik Ramadani. I am originally from Albania," another shallow inhalation breath, "but now I live in America a few blocks from your building. I walk by here every day to go to the corner market," another puff on his nebulizer.

"Okay," said one.

"Several days ago, I was walking by when I heard a lot of racket within your establishment." He stopped and took as deep of breath as possible. "Too much smoking," he gasped, leaning on his cane, his shoulders hunched as his head gave slight jerking movements. "I looked inside just as that large metal cylinder appeared out of thin air and landed and scraped along on the cement floor. A few minutes later, you three exited along with that black Terrier. The dog's collar reads JJ Astor IV. The animal is over 110 years old and should have died in 1912 along with his owner, Mr. Astor, If I'm not mistaken, but you brought him back with you after visiting the Titanic. Correct?" he waited and watched and tried to control his breathing. He pulled out an inhaler from his pocket and took two more puffs. "Better," he said.

The teenage scientists stood quietly and waited for the other shoe to drop.

"I read a great deal, for I have nothing else to do after my wife died. I have read numerous articles about the Titanic going down over a hundred years ago, and on that ship was Astor and his dog."

The four glanced in the corner where the dog was sleeping quietly.

"I think you have built a time machine, and that is what I need. Last year my Amelia went to the corner market. A bad man came into the store and demanded money. He did not get as much as he wanted, so he killed Mr. Chin, the owner, and his wife, Mrs. Chin. Unfortunately, my wife, Amelia, was there too, and he killed her as well. It was horrible!"

"Perhaps you should come in, for it is starting to rain," said Joyce guiding the elderly man while pointing to a ragged overstuffed chair on the far side of the building.

At first, there was a slight sprinkle; but soon it became a steady mist which quickly became a heavy drizzle from the dark clouds. The downpour pounded on the laboratory's tin roof, making a hellish noise as if a child was learning to play the cymbals and not doing a good job.

"Would you care for a cup of hot tea, Mr. Ramadani?" questioned Joyce as she headed for the stove where she had water boiling. "It's chilly in this old building. Therefore, we always have the hot water ready."

"That would be nice," he coughed. "It is so kind of you to offer. I don't have many friends now that my Amelia is gone. She was my wife, but a friend too," he was able to say before tears flooded his eyes, and he got choked up, which started him wheezing again. His whole body grew rigid, and he was reduced to silence as he caught his breath and was able to breathe again. His eyes darted suspiciously around the large room as he projected a faint smile.

"So, Mr..." started Washington.

"Please call me, Ben; it is easier to say," another false grin, a clearing of his throat and a cough.

"So, Ben, you believe we three teenagers built a time machine in this dirty room? In this old, and dilapidated building, when the world's most brilliant scientists have never been able to accomplish this task?"

He bobbed his head positive.

"Please finish your tea, Ben, and come back tomorrow, and maybe we'll discuss our plans to visit Mars and Venus next week." Washington turned away smiling and shook his head.

CHAPTER 25

"Well," began Washington, "what the hell are we going to do now?" he asked as he got up, went over by the stove, and poured himself a cup of tea. "Any cream?"

Joyce shook her head negatively.

"Maybe we should help the old guy," stated John tilting his head. "Or kill the sucker; no one would miss him!"

"Be serious, John!" ordered his sister, scowling.

"Let's say we help him save his wife from being murdered. Is that even possible, or are we screwing around with Mother Nature? And as you both know, you don't fool with Mother Nature."

"We brought Scotty back with us."

"Yeah, but he wasn't dead yet. We bring them back alive, or we don't bring them back at all!" giggled Eddie at the joke, but the other two were silent. "Okay, we take him back. But what if he comes back the following week and wants us to save his mother, who's been dead for 30 years, and then his dad, or maybe his favorite cat or something? Are we opening a can of worms that can crawl out and strangle us to death?"

The old building was quiet except for the rat-tat-tat of heavy pellets of rain continuing to bang on the old metal roof.

"I have to pee," said Joyce hurrying to the bathroom.

"What do you think, John? Are we making a mistake or saving a little old man from loneliness in his few remaining years?"

"I don't know," said Joyce, hearing the question,

"Neither do I," answered John staring at the floor as if he had lost a contact lens.

"Well, crap! Maybe we should help the poor bastard!"

"Okay, but with the understanding, he will never tell a soul how we helped him or ask for our services again."

"But what if he does? Are we going to have all of the Albanian immigrants banging on our door for our... ah, services, as he called them? I checked Google, and there are over 60,000 Albanians in New York. So, you can imagine our dilemma if he tells even one of his Albanian relatives or friends. That knowledge would spread like wildfire!"

"We will tell him if he does, we will go back and not save his wife, Amelia. That should take the wind out of his sails if he gets any bright ideas."

"You always talk tough, but we know you're a wuss." The trio laughed at each other, for they all knew they would help him no matter what.

CHAPTER 26

The old Albanian sat down and waited. They told him of their decision and concerns and what would happen if he even told a single person. His eyes widened after hearing they would undo his wife returning. He nodded his head continually.

"We need the date and hour when all of that happened," said Washington, preparing to write in on his iPad.

"It was Monday, 6:37 p.m., when a police officer called me and said my wife had just be killed at Chin's Market. So, either we get there before it happens or..."

"Before it happens, obviously," stated Washington.

"Is everybody belted in?" asked the craft's pilot as he prepared the craft for takeoff adjusting the many dials and nobs. "Hold on, troops!"

There was a loud crackling sound, intense shaking and deep rumbling noises. Zap, they were gone.

A second later, they were back in the lab, but it was now Monday, 6:25 p.m.

They crawled out of the craft, and Ben quickly hurried to the door. Just at that moment, an elderly, grey-haired woman, with a brightly colored scarf around her head was walking by as he came out of the building.

"Besnik Ramadani, what on earth were you doing in there?" she bristled in her foreign tongue. "That is someone else's building!" she scolded.

"We asked him to come in and have some tea," said Joyce. "I'm Joyce Wilson, and that's my brother, John, over there is Edward Washington. Would you join us for a quick cup of hot tea, Mrs. Ramadani?"

"Please call me, Amelia," she answered in broken English. "It is getting chilly outside, and tea sounds good," she smiled.

They all looked at their watches. They read *6:38* p.m. They heard sirens and saw flashing red and yellow light as several police cars raced by.

"Besnik, you've been acting so strange. Have you been shopping on Amazon again, you bad boy?" she patted Ben's leg and smiled a love caring smile. She looked at the three and said, "Besnik likes to buy things on the internet. He forgets they cost money. So, I must keep an eye on him otherwise he will drive us into bankruptcy for his spending on Amazon."

John, Joyce and Edward chuckled.

Ben looked at the three and bowed his head several times. "Thank you," he whispered smirking.

They nodded back.

CHAPTER 27

"One more time for the Gipper?" questioned Washington as he sat at the control waiting.

His two colleagues looked perplexed.

"You teenage geniuses don't know about the Gipper? Brother! Let me enlighten you two. George Gipp, The Gipper, was a Notre Dame star football player under Knute Rockne a long time ago. He died extremely young, but during halftime, while Notre Dame was playing Army, the Coach said to his team, 'Let's win one more time for the Gipper,' and they did."

"That's sad," complained Joyce.

"Yeah, but true. So, one more time for the Gipper?" questioned Washington as he sat at the controls and waited, ginning ear to ear.

"Why not," they echoed.

A moment later, they were gone.

CHAPTER 28

A re we headed back home?" questioned Joyce, looking over toward her brother and back to Edward. She was feeling edgy and did not know why.

This diversional trip was far into the unknown. It was a soft summer breeze while standing on the beach in the dead of winter, a scrap on the floor in a dark room, regaining consciousness from a general anesthetic; it was an eerie feeling of déjà vu.

Each felt the strangeness flow over them as if going under the water. It was as if someone walked over their grave before they had been interred.

"I don't like where you are taking us, Edward," barked John Wilson as he too was felt the odd sensation. "Take us home, Eddie!"

And then they landed. The three quickly took to the portholes. The craft had landed on a steep rocky slope near a large walled village. Below were numerous people lined up as if waiting for a parade or something. The women were wearing veils, and long flowing robes, as did the men, and both wore sandals. Some wore short, knee-length tunic. Several men were military, for they wore strips of armor and wool tunics with helmets, and swords wore high on the right side of the body; others carried spears.

"Where are we?" the twins asked again. The screen has gone blank, which is odd.

"Wrap a blanket around you so we won't stand out so much!" ordered Washington.

The other two followed his orders but thought it strange how he was acting.

"Let's go," he said, opening the hatch and crawling out.

They made their way slowly down the steep hill walking by other people. The three heard small talk about a Jew who had been condemned by the Pontius Pilate and was being tortured and was scheduled to be crucified between two thieves. They called the man; King of the Jews, and he was ordered to carry a cross outside Jerusalem, where he was to be crucified.

"Did you hear that?"

"We all did. Are you thinking what I'm thinking?"

"They are talking about Jesus Christ."

There was a loud murmuring sound of the crowd as they watched a beaten and bleeding man wearing nothing but a loincloth after a soldier tore off his robe. Some of the people were spitting on him; others were casting stones. While some dropped to their knees, weeping and trying to tough the dying soul.

The mob of onlookers watched as soldiers occasionally struck him in the face with sticks of wood or their spears. The viewers could see his battered, bruised body had deep lacerations on his back and legs. One soldier took a flagrum whip and struck the man's shoulders repeatedly with all of his might.

The three put their hands to their mouths in aw when they saw the tortured man, who was in obvious pain, attempt to lift a huge wooden cross to his shoulders and continue to drag it. The rough wood of the beam gouged his already lacerated skin and muscles of the shoulders. He struggled with the cross and dropped to his knees again. It was at this time Edward raced out and helped him up.

With tears in his eyes, Jesus turned to him and whispered, "Edward, let them do what they must."

About this time, a Centurion knocked Washington long the side of his head with his heavy spear stunning the traveler, but Washington was able to crawl back to the side of the road.

"What did he say?" they both asked.

"Edward, let them do what they must."

"He knew your name?

He nodded.

"It's Jesus Christ!" they all said together, never taking their eyes off what was happening on The Via Dolorosa, or 'the way of sorrow' as it is now called, which is a stone street in Jerusalem.

The soldiers mocked him by placing a stick in his hand as a scepter and a crown of thorns on his head while laughing as his head bled.

"They will crucify him," whimpered Joyce with tears streaming down her cheeks.

"They crucified him 2000 years ago."

"I don't think we should watch."

"We don't either."

Jesus suffered and was crucified outside the city's wall at Golgotha. He died after being nailed to the cross that he carried.

His last words were, "Father, forgive them for they know not what they do."

He was 33 years old.

CHAPTER 29

The return to normalcy was difficult for the three after what they had been through. Therefore, the trio decided to wait a certain amount of time before reentering the time capsule.

And today was that time...

The End

www.ingramcontent.com/pod-product-compliance
Lightning Source LLC
Chambersburg PA
CBHW022134150726

47992CB00002B/586